THE TRANSFORMERS™—
Robots
in Disguise!

They came from Cybertron—a planet of
machines—where war raged for thousands of years
between the noble Autobots and the evil
Decepticons.

NOW THE BATTLE OF THESE POWERFUL
ROBOTS IS YOUR BATTLE!

ONLY YOU can protect the earth from the evil
destruction of the Decepticons!

Read the directions at the bottom of each page.
Then decide what the Autobots should do next.

If you decide correctly, the Autobots will triumph!
If you make the wrong choices, the unspeakable
evil of the Decepticons will rule the world!

Hurry! The adventure begins on page 1.

Find Your Fate™ Junior Transformers™ #4

THE TRANSFORMERS™

Earthquake

by Ann Matthews

BALLANTINE BOOKS • NEW YORK

Library of Congress Catalog Card Number: 85-91167

ISBN: 0-345-33071-4

Editorial Services by Parachute Press, Inc.

Illustrated by William Schmidt

Designed by Gene Siegel

Manufactured in the United States of America

First Edition: April 1986

10 9 8 7 6 5 4 3 2 1

THE TRANSFORMERS™

Earthquake

It is a quiet day in the Autobot headquarters, hidden deep within the hills near Center City, Oregon. Optimus Prime, leader of the brave and peace-loving alien robots, glances around at the pulsing machinery, monitoring devices, and electrical equipment that make up headquarters. "What a pleasant change," he says. "No fighting for once."

"Yeah," agrees Beachcomber, who always yearns for the quiet life. He settles back in a lounge chair. "It's wonderful when the Decepticons are laying low."

"It gives me a chance to polish up my gorgeous body," says the vain Sunstreaker, buffing his back.

"And *I* can stay in shape," says Brawn, working out on the special circuitry-building equipment. "Strength is the only way to keep those evil robots in their places."

"Sometimes a little trickery helps," says Mirage with a mischievous grin. "I can get to those Decepticons every time when I project my image and appear to be where I'm not!"

"I wish the Decepticons *would* show up," boasts Powerglide. "I'd teach them a thing or two."

"Well, don't worry," answers Cosmos. "We're about due for another attack. The last one was at least . . . two days ago."

Turn to page 2.

1

"You know what I'd like to do?" Beachcomber says. "I'd like to forget about the Decepticons, transform into my dune buggy mode, and take a long drive."

"Yeah. That's one thing the Decepticons can't do," says Sunstreaker. "When *they* abandon their robot form, they turn into missiles and planes."

"I think you should have the day off, Beachcomber," says Optimus Prime. "You deserve it."

And that's exactly what Beachcomber does. Within a few minutes, he's left headquarters and has transformed into his dune buggy mode. He heads into the countryside.

The road Beachcomber is driving on slowly becomes rougher and rockier. Soon he turns onto a dirt lane and just jounces through the countryside.

After a while, Beachcomber pulls to a stop beneath a tall pine tree. He listens. He can't hear a sound except for a lone bird crying. *This is the life,* thinks the Autobot. *No wars, no fighting. Just plenty of silence and beautiful land.* . . . Suddenly—rumble, rumble, *BOOM!*

Beachcomber feels the ground shake beneath his wheels with a terrifying force. It feels like the whole earth is breaking apart. What's happening?

. . . .

Go on to page 3 and find out.

Beachcomber gets moving, trying to find out what's making the earth shake. Pulling up behind some boulders, he peers around, trying to discover some clue.

Suddenly Beachcomber spots a movement. It looks like . . . the Decepticon Rumble. Rumble is small but tough and can cause powerful earthquakes with the low-frequency groundwaves he creates.

Beachcomber watches Rumble. It looks as if he's practicing. *But,* Beachcomber thinks suspiciously, *why would he need to do that? Maybe the Decepticons are planning something big!*

After a few more small earthquakes, Rumble saunters proudly away and begins to climb up a cliff. Beachcomber follows from a safe distance.

Soon Rumble pauses in front of a sheer cliff face. Suddenly, as if by magic, a huge double door hidden in the cliff opens just long enough for him to enter.

Beachcomber realizes that he's found the Decepticons' hidden fortress! He wants to report back to Optimus Prime, but he's afraid that if he leaves, he might not be able to find this remote location again. Maybe he should investigate the Decepticon fortress himself immediately. What do you think?

. . . .

If you think Beachcomber should hurry back to Autobot headquarters, turn to page 5.

If you decide Beachcomber's best move would be to enter the fortress alone, turn to page 62.

3

"Information about what?" Megatron growls, but Cosmos sees an eagerness in his eyes. Cosmos quickly tells Megatron about Starscream and Soundwave's conversation in the generator room. He plays up the nasty parts for drama.

As Megatron listens, he begins to tremble with rage. "Traitors!" he roars. Without a second glance at Cosmos, he strides into the generator room. Cosmos, alone in the corridor now, hears his nuclear-charged fusion cannon go off. The fortress seems to shake at its very core.

Then Cosmos hears footsteps. He ducks behind an open door as Decepticons run toward the generator room from all over the fortress. "Are you *all* traitors?" cries Megatron.

Some of the Decepticons rush to their leader's side, but others are clearly with Soundwave and Starscream. Instantly, fighting breaks out and spills into the corridor near Cosmos.

Cosmos knows that a Decepticon mutiny is no place for a lone Autobot. He races through flying bullets and showers of glass and metal debris. As he leaves the sounds of the battle behind him, he runs smack into Sunstreaker. Quickly he explains what has happened.

"That's great," exclaims the Autobot warrior, "because we've found the lab! Come on!"

. . . .
Follow Sunstreaker and Cosmos to page 33.

Beachcomber knows this is no job for one lone Autobot. He scans the cliff through which Rumble has disappeared and tries to memorize its every feature so he can recognize it later. Then he quickly returns to the dirt road and follows it, at top speed, back to Autobot headquarters.

Home again, Beachcomber transforms to his robot mode, steps into headquarters, and calls to Optimus Prime.

"Beachcomber!" exclaims the Autobot leader. "Back so soon? What happened to your day off?"

"We've got trouble," announces Beachcomber. "I found the Decepticons' fortress and they're up to something. Rumble was outside creating earthquakes. It smells pretty fishy to me, so I think we better get over there and investigate."

"Good work, Beachcomber!" says Optimus Prime. "And now you've got a chance to do more good work. I want you, Powerglide, and Windcharger to go back to the fortress and look around. See what you can find out. But be careful. You know that Decepticons are ruthless!"

There's no time to lose! Turn to page 6.

Outside of headquarters, the three Autobots quickly travel through the countryside toward the isolated cliffs.

"Okay," says Beachcomber. "This is it, the Decepticons' fortress." He faces the cliff wall. "The door is right there." He points to what looks like sheer rock to the others.

"Where?" asks Powerglide.

"It's there. Just believe me," replies Beachcomber.

"How are we going to get inside?" asks Windcharger.

"They same way Rumble did," answers Powerglide.

"Will the door open for an Autobot?" wonders Beachcomber. "Maybe we should investigate outside. I could examine the cliffs with my sensors. I might be able to find another way in."

"Sure," agrees Powerglide, "but that will take longer. Who knows what the Decepticons are doing in there. We might not have much time."

"But going through the Decepticons' front door could lead us into big trouble," replies Beachcomber.

The Autobots can't make the decision alone. They need your help!

. . . .

If you think Beachcomber and the others should try to enter through the main door of the fortress, turn to page 10.

If you think they should search for another entrance to the fortress, turn to page 8.

Inside the Decepticons' lab, there's a large panel full of buttons and levers.

"Have a seat, make yourselves at home," Megatron commands Beachcomber and Buster. "Now sit back and watch that radar screen. The bull's-eye is Center City and the black line headed toward it is the Destruction Beam."

Beachcomber lunges for the panel and manages to punch the button before Megatron and the others can stop him. He waits for the Destruction Beam to stop and . . .

Nothing happens!

"Valiant effort, Autobot," Megatron says sarcastically, "but that panel is a fake. The real control button is over there." He points to a metal shape on the wall across the room. "Now sit down and enjoy the show!" Megatron pushes Beachcomber roughly into a chair.

Starscream starts counting. "Five, four, three, two one. . . ." Horrified, Beachcomber and Buster watch the Destruction Beam make contact with Center City.

"And now," Megatron says, "Rumble is outside Center City. He will send a few groundwaves to set the earthquake in motion."

He pulls out his nuclear-powered fusion cannon. "As a parting thought," he adds, "you won't be dying alone. In less than two hours, London, Paris, Washington, D. C., and Moscow will all be gone, too. Sweet dreams!"

Megatron pulls the trigger!

THE END

The Autobots turn away from the fortress door. As they scout around the cliffs and rocks, Beachcomber's sensors study the terrain, looking for any opening in the solid wall.

Windcharger spots a break in the cliff. "What's this?" he calls. He crawls inside the narrow gap. Powerglide follows him, but they come back out a few seconds later. It's a small cave.

The Autobots continue to search until Beachcomber cries, "Okay, I think I've got something!" His sensors have detected a narrow passageway into the cliff, hidden by bushes and scrub brush. "I'll bet the Decepticons didn't know *this* was here when they took over the cliff for their fortress," he says. He slips through the opening and the others follow.

Turn to page 64.

Windcharger faces the towering cliff. "Open sesame," he says. Like magic, the double doors slide open and Windcharger dashes forward. But before he's completely inside, the heavy doors slam shut, crushing him to a heap of smoking metal.

Then, in a flash, the doors open again and a swarm of Decepticons flies out. Beachcomber thinks fast. There's only one way out of this. "I sure hope Rumble doesn't start an earthquake!" he shouts to Powerglide.

"Ha! Fool!" cries Rumble cockily. He sends out a massive groundwave. *R-R-UMBLE!* The earth is ripped open . . . right underneath the Decepticon fortress.

"Just what we needed!" cheers Beachcomber. As the fortress caves in, the Autobots make a run for it. Behind them they hear the shouts of the evil Decepticons as they helplessly watch their home disappear.

When they're far away from the Decepticons, the Autobots stop to catch their electronic breath. "We can go back for Windcharger once the dust settles," says Beachcomber. "Medical Officer Ratchet will fix him up."

"Yeah. That Rumble sure crumbled everything!" says Powerglide. "I don't think we'll have to worry about the Decepticons for a while. The world is safe— at least for another twenty-four hours!"

THE END

Beachcomber and Windcharger watch Powerglide dash off, then they reenter the storage room. Windcharger points to the other passageway. "It might lead us around the outside of the fortress," he whispers. "Then we could gather information without being seen."

Beachcomber nods. "Let's go," he says.

The Autobots start down the passageway. They haven't gone far when it ends abruptly in a heavy stone doorway. Yellow light shines from the crack beneath it. From somewhere comes the sound of voices—Decepticon voices. But the voices are very faint. Is the enemy on the other side of the door or are they farther away?

"Let's go in," says Windcharger, reaching for the door.

Beachcomber holds back. "No way! We could walk right into a nest of Decepticons. We'd never get out alive."

"We're armed," Windcharger points out, "and they wouldn't be expecting us. We'd have the advantage."

"Going in is suicide," says Beachcomber.

The Autobots are never going to resolve this argument. You better help them.

. . . .

If you get the feeling that opening the door is risky and you think Beachcomber should go back to the storage room, turn to page 13.

If you think it's safe for the Autobots to go ahead, turn to page 24.

11

Hidden in Megatron's elaborate spy station, Beachcomber and Windcharger hear Decepticon voices—and they're growing louder.

"The Destruction Beam just left the lab," announces Frenzy.

"Very good," replies Megatron. "Those meddling Autobots don't know a thing about it. My plan can't help but succeed!"

The door opens and Megatron steps into the room. He leaves Frenzy outside and the door swings shut. In a flash, the Autobots jump out from behind the computers and grab the Decepticon leader. Windcharger disarms him by creating a magnetic field which attracts all of the evil ruler's weapons.

"The fortress is surrounded, Megatron," Beachcomber bluffs. "Every single Autobot is waiting outside. You are just the first to be captured. If you don't want to see this entire fortress blown to bits, with you and your Decepticons in it, I suggest you order your men to surrender. Then show us your lab so we can keep the Destruction Beam from reaching Center City."

Megatron thinks he has no choice. While he addresses the Decepticons over the loudspeaker, Beachcomber pulls out his communicator and transmits an urgent message to Optimus Prime, telling him to send the Autobots.

An hour later, Center City still stands—but the Decepticons have fallen.

THE END

12

"Forget it, Windcharger," says Beachcomber as he and his friend stand before the strange stone door. "I'm not going in there."

"See you later, then," says Windcharger. He turns toward the door as Beachcomber retreats down the passage.

Several seconds later, Beachcomber is back in the storage room. Now what? He doesn't really want to explore the fortress alone. Maybe there's still time to catch up with Powerglide.

Cautiously, he opens the door into the fortress. He steps into the silent, cold corridor and . . .

A huge metal hand clamps down on Beachcomber's arm.

Beachcomber struggles. Then a familiar voice says, "Calm down, it's me."

"Powerglide! What are you doing here?"

"Looking for you. I wanted company."

"Okay," says Beachcomber. "I'm ready. But let's be careful."

Beachcomber and Powerglide head quietly down the corridor.

. . . .

Follow them and turn to page 20.

13

Beachcomber bolts through the entrance and just squeezes by before the massive doors quickly slide together. "Piece of cake!" he says.

But Beachcomber should know by now not to get cocky around Decepticons. As he rushes into the fortress, the cruel Buzzsaw leaps on him from a hidden ledge.

"Gotcha!" Buzzsaw exclaims. *R-i-i-i-p! Screech!* Instantly, the Decepticon's diamond-hard, knifelike beak carves the unsuspecting Autobot into metal ribbons.

Then Scrapper moves in and takes Beachcomber apart. He doesn't stop until he has found and carefully saved the Autobot's memory circuits. Scrapper piles the pieces of Beachcomber into his arms and takes them to Megatron, the Decepticons' leader.

"Ah," says Megatron softly, his cold eyes shining as he fingers Beachcomber's circuits. "A good job, Decepticons. Let's play these and see what we have."

Once they've studied Beachcomber's metallic brain, the Decepticons know all top-secret, confidential Autobot information. Then Megatron hatches an evil plan. . . .

Find out just how evil it is on page 19.

Beachcomber and Powerglide are in a pretty tight spot—caught in a corridor with no place to hide and Decepticons too close for comfort.

Beachcomber recognizes one of the voices as that of Megatron, ruler of the Decepticons. It is coming from a room off the hallway and he sounds completely crazy. "My plan," he says, "cannot fail, and when it is completed the world will be free of humans at last. Imagine, Soundwave, the earth will become a massive laboratory for my experiments. We'll use the entire planet as a launching pad so that the Decepticons can return to Cybertron and claim what is rightfully ours."

"The war is on," Soundwave says coldly.

"Then the Destruction Beam is on its way? And is Rumble in place and ready to send the groundwaves that will crack Center City?"

"The Destruction Beam just left the lab, and Rumble is ready. In one hour, fifty-two minutes, and thirty-seven seconds, Center City, Oregon, will look like the dark side of the moon," Soundwave assures him.

"Ah," says Megatron thoughtfully. "The first to go. A little test. If it's successful, New York, Los Angeles, Chicago, Houston, and Washington, D. C., will follow. Then other cities in every part of the world. It's so simple, but it's a stroke of genius. . . ."

The Autobots stare at each other in horror. They don't have a second to waste!

. . . .

Hurry and go on to page 17.

Beachcomber and Powerglide race back to the fortress's secret entrance and find Windcharger already there. In half a second, all three are outside the fortress and transformed into their vehicular modes.

The Autobots waste no time getting back to headquarters. Breathlessly, they call Optimus Prime and the others together and explain Megatron's mad, ruthless plot.

"The Destruction Beam is already on its way!" cries Powerglide. "It should reach Center City in about an hour and a half."

"We can stop it," says Optimus Prime calmly. "We *must* stop it. We *will* stop it! Autobots, transform and let's get to that fortress!"

"But shouldn't we go to Center City?" asks Windcharger. "Rumble is probably there preparing to split the fault created by the Destruction Beam and cause an earthquake. We may not be able to stop the fault line from being created, but we can stop Rumble."

He has a point. "All right," says Optimus Prime. "I'll organize a lead team of the most powerful Autobots to go to one location, and a smaller team can go to the other." He pauses, thinking.

Cosmos asks the question everyone is wondering about. "But where should the lead team go? To the fortress to demolish the lab or to the city?"

. . . .

If you think the lead team should go to the fortress, turn to page 68.

If you're certain the lead team should go to Center City, turn to page 36.

17

Beachcomber studies the code for a few minutes. Suddenly he snaps his fingers. "I think I've got it. It's a simple code, really. Each number stands for a letter of the alphabet: 1 equals A, 2 is B, and so forth. Here, I'll write it down for you." He uses his finger to write in the dirt floor.

16/21/19/8—18/5/4—2/21/20/20/15/14

PUSH RED BUTTON

"Red button?" says Windcharger. He and Beachcomber begin feeling around the door.

"Here it is," says Windcharger. The button is hidden by a piece of loose rock next to the doorjamb. "Should I push it?"

"Why not?" replies Beachcomber. "The code and the button were put here by a Decepticon for another Decepticon. It can't be a trap, because they'd never expect an Autobot to be here. We'll take them by surprise like you said . . . I hope."

"Here goes nothing," says Windcharger. He pushes the button.

. . . .

Turn to page 25.

18

Megatron sorts through the junk that was once Beachcomber. "Bring me Mixmaster and Hook, the Constructicons," he commands. When they arrive, Megatron orders them to rebuild Beachcomber.

"Make sure you switch this memory chip for the Autobot's old one," Megatron orders, and hands two almost identical chips to Hook.

The Constructicons work quickly, re-creating Beachcomber's original form. At last, they're ready to insert the memory chip. "Which one do we use?" asks Mixmaster uncertainly.

"The Destructicon chip, of course," snaps Hook.

When the work is done, Megatron looks upon the perfect undercover agent—the body of a trusted Autobot with the dastardly mind of a Decepticon. Then he sends him back to Autobot headquarters.

"I'm back!" Beachcomber announces, striding into the Autobot hideout. Quickly, he recaps his big adventure to Optimus Prime and the others. "And guess what?" he says, coming to the end of his story. "Those bungling Constructicons put my *old* memory chip back in by mistake. What's more, Megatron told me all his plans."

Optimus Prime laughs long and hard. "With you as a double agent, we'll be able to dismantle Megatron's entire operation."

Beachcomber sighs happily. "We'll be home on Cybertron soon!"

THE END

As Beachcomber and Powerglide sneak down the corridor, they pause at each doorway and listen. Nothing. The fortress is strangely silent. Why? Can it really be full of Decepticons? It sure doesn't feel like it. Are the Autobots walking into an ambush or is the element of surprise on their side? Beachcomber shakes his head in confusion.

At the end of the corridor, Powerglide comes to an abrupt halt and Beachcomber nearly runs into him. Powerglide signals him to listen. And suddenly Beachcomber hears the sound too—Decepticon voices!

To find out what they're saying, turn to page 16.

Beachcomber backs away from the entrance in the cliff face. He figures that if the doors opened for him once, they'll probably open a second time. And those human voices he heard aren't going to wait. He decides to transform into his vehicular mode again. The humans would be suspicious if they saw a robot. In an instant, he looks like just another dune buggy.

Beachcomber bounces over the rocky terrain, sending up clouds of dust. All at once, he rounds a towering boulder and finds himself face to face with two humans—Buster and Jessie!

"Beachcomber?" Buster asks. "Is that you?"

"It sure is," Beachcomber says, glad to see his human friends instead of the ominous strangers he'd expected. Buster's father, Sparkplug, is a friend of the Autobots.

"Boy, am I happy you're here!" exclaims Buster.

"We were exploring," says Jessie breathlessly, "and guess what happened!"

"We stumbled onto the Decepticons' fortress," Buster relates breathlessly. "It's inside this cliff, and we found a secret passageway to it! We overheard Megatron explaining his new plan. It's just awful. The Decepticons are going to take over the *world!*"

Turn to page 22—the bad news isn't over yet!

Buster tells Beachcomber that the Decepticons have invented something they call a Destruction Beam. "Laserbeak sends it underground from a Decepticon lab hidden in this cliff," he explains. "It creates a crack in the ground like a fault line. The Decepticons plan to have Rumble use his earthquake-making powers to split the crack wide open."

"They are testing it," adds Jessie. "They've just sent a beam to Center City. It's due to hit in an hour and a half!"

Beachcomber tells Buster and Jessie to hop in. He wants to drive them back to Autobot headquarters so they can tell Optimus Prime what they've learned. But they don't get far.

Down from the sky swoops a white and red fighter jet, the Decepticon Ramjet in his jet form. He lands next to the dune buggy, firing at it. Suddenly Ramjet transforms into his robot mode and scoops up Jessie. Then he turns back into a jet and flies off with her.

Beachcomber wants to return immediately to Autobot headquarters to get help. Buster argues with Beachcomber. "We can't leave without Jessie!" he shouts.

· ·

If you want them to go back to the Decepticon fortress to attempt to find Jessie, turn to page 26.

If you think they should get help, turn to page 32.

22

"All right," says Beachcomber with a sigh, "how do you propose we get in there?"

"Bust the door down!" cries Windcharger impatiently, eager for excitement. He can smash through it in a jiffy by casting one of his powerful magnetic fields.

"Wait!" says Beachcomber suddenly. "Look." He points to the top of the door. There's a lighted panel with what looks like a list of numbers on it. Here's what the Autobots see:

16/21/19/8—18/5/4—2/21/20/20/15/14

"What is it?" asks Windcharger.

"Some kind of code, I guess," replies Beachcomber. "If we can crack it, we'll be able to get through that door. What do you know about codes?"

"Not much," admits Windcharger.

Can you help the Autobots?

. . . .

If you can crack the code, give yourself a pat on the back and turn to page 18.

If the code is a mystery to you, turn to page 65.

The door swings open and the two Autobots flatten themselves against the wall. They listen but hear nothing. Finally, Windcharger peers into the room beyond. "Hey, look at this!" he exclaims.

The room is lavishly furnished with all sorts of electronic equipment—viewing screens, recording devices, voice monitors, computers, and transmitters. It's obviously a spy station, but the corridors shown on the screens are the fortress's own. A thick red carpet covers the floor, and a massive metal desk stands in one corner. Windcharger and Beachcomber step inside. The door swings shut behind them.

"Wow! What a place," says Beachcomber.

"I'll bet this is Megatron's secret chamber," says Windcharger. "Only he would feel the need to spy on his own people. I'm sure that's what he does from here."

"Shhh!" says Beachcomber suddenly. "Someone's coming."

"Quick!" whispers Windcharger. "Hide."

Beachcomber and Windcharger duck behind a bank of computer screens and wait. . . .

. . . .

Shhh. Turn to page 12.

"Okay, we'll go after Jessie," says Beachcomber, flooring the gas pedal. "We'd never get to headquarters and back in less than an hour and a half anyway."

Beachcomber speeds toward the fortress. "Our only chance is to face the Decepticons ourselves," he declares.

"*Fat* chance!" cries Buster. "But at least I can find Jessie. There's no way I'm leaving her with those despicable Decepticons."

"And we've got another problem," cries Beachcomber. "We can't use the entrance I found. Megatron and the others will be expecting us. If we walk in the front door, they'll wipe us out. I'll wind up in an auto-body shop!"

"No problem," says Buster. "I found that secret passage once, and I can find it again. We'll sneak inside the fortress without tripping a single alarm.

"Turn left," Buster orders. "Now right. Now left again. Okay, here it is." Buster and Beachcomber stand outside the black wall of a looming, gloomy cliff.

"I don't see anything," says Beachcomber.

"It's right here," says Buster. "Now hurry up and transform."

. . . .

While Beachcomber is changing into his robot mode, go on to page 27.

Buster leads Beachcomber behind a large round boulder. "This is the secret entrance to the Decepticons' fortress," he whispers, pointing to a narrow passage in the cliff wall. He and Beachcomber hurry into it.

The passage grows darker and colder until it ends in an evil-smelling little cave. Beachcomber and Buster are faced with another stone wall.

Buster smiles at Beachcomber's confusion. "This wall is really a door." He pushes a hidden lever and the rock wall swings inward. "Come on," he says.

Beachcomber and Buster sneak into the Decepticons' fortress. But they're not two steps past the door when Buster stops suddenly. "I hear voices," he says.

"The Decepticons!" whispers Beachcomber. "We'd better hide!"

"No," says Buster. "One of the voices is Jessie's. Let's follow her."

"We'll get caught."

"We've got to save Jessie," says Buster. "And the people of Center City need us to act and act fast. We've *got* to go on! *Now!*"

What would you do?

. . . .

If you would follow the voices, turn to page 46 . . . quietly.

If you'd rather hide, turn to page 49.

Cosmos stands stock-still in the middle of the corridor. There's no place for him to hide from whoever just opened that door. Luckily, the Decepticons don't venture into the hallway. Cosmos does, however, hear a low voice. Deciding to investigate, he follows the sounds to the fortress's generator. The Decepticons Starscream and Soundwave are there, nervously pacing back and forth. Cosmos slips into the room unnoticed and hides behind a large piece of machinery.

"My plan would be easy," says Starscream. "Megatron is getting too cocky about this plan of his. He's becoming careless. He forgets to change the coded number lock to his secret chambers. I know how to get in."

"Hmmm," says Soundwave. "That *is* easy. We simply wait for him in his room. Then, when he comes in, I stun him with a gamma ray—and we become the new leaders of the Decepticons."

Cosmos has heard enough. He sneaks out of the generator room . . . and bumps right into Megatron. Cosmos is shaking in his metallic boots as he confronts the Decepticons' leader.

Before Megatron can make a move to smash him, Cosmos says, "I've got a little information for you. I'm sure you'd be interested."

How do you think Megatron will react?

. . . .

If you think he'd believe Cosmos, turn to page 4.
If you think he wouldn't believe Cosmos, turn to page 39.

"All right," Megatron snarls, "this is the lab." He pushes open an unmarked door and the Autobots find themselves in the largest lab they've ever seen.

Megatron crosses the room to a radar screen. A line of red light is slowly working its way across the screen toward a bull's-eye in the center.

"That's the Destruction Beam," Megatron says proudly. "It's ten minutes from Center City now."

"Stop it," orders Optimus Prime.

Megatron stares at him but doesn't move a muscle.

Beachcomber spots a button under the radar screen and pushes it. The red line stops moving—then slowly fades away.

"Center City is safe," says Optimus Prime with relief. "And the Decepticons are going down in history as a bunch of losers!" He takes careful aim with his laser rifle and blows the Destruction Beam machine to robot heaven.

Most of the Decepticons are permanently maimed in battle, and the Autobots leave the fortress victoriously, taking Megatron with them. But back at headquarters they have to trade him for the release of several of their own kind, since the Autobots in Center City were badly beaten by the Decepticons.

"They'll be back making more trouble," Optimus Prime says, "but for now, well, let's all sit back and recharge."

THE END

"Cosmos, you're absolutely right," Optimus Prime says. "Humans definitely aren't ready for spaceships. You know, they'd probably think we were invading aliens if they saw you."

Optimus Prime opens his rear doors and Cosmos happily flies out of the truck. He soars skyward and zooms back in the direction from which the Autobots have just come. *What a way to go,* he thinks. *Give me wings any day. Who needs wheels? They just slow the world down.*

Cosmos whizzes along and soon reaches the deserted hills. He uses his communicator to ask Smokescreen for the coordinates of the fortress. In a flash he's there and looking for the smaller team of Autobots.

But the Autobots are nowhere in sight. The double doors to the fortress stand wide open. "What a welcome," says Cosmos. "Waiting for me with open doors!" He makes a bumpy landing in the soft, sandy soil and pauses in front of the cliff, listening and waiting. He doesn't hear a sound. He tries communicating with Smokescreen, but nothing happens.

Cosmos transforms into his robot form and cautiously steps through the doors into the fortress beyond. Are the other Autobots inside? Why can't he rouse Smokescreen on his communicator? *If they're not here,* he thinks, *it's up to me to save the world.* He starts down a corridor.

Suddenly Cosmos hears a door creak open.

· ·

Ready, aim, fire onto page 28.

"I can't believe we're leaving Jessie back there!" exclaims Buster as he and Beachcomber drive away from the Decepticon fortress.

"We need help," replies Beachcomber as he speeds along. "There's no way we can save Jessie without the other Autobots with us, and we sure can't stop Megatron's foul Destruction Beam alone. But, Buster, don't worry. We'll save Jessie. Besides, the Decepticons aren't going to do anything to her. She's more useful to them alive than dead."

"Great," mutters Buster.

By breaking the speed limit, Buster and Beachcomber reach the Autobot headquarters in less than twenty minutes. They explain everything to Optimus Prime and the other robots—the whole story of the secret entrance to the fortress, the Destruction Beam aimed at Center City, and Jessie's capture.

"Those . . . those CREEPS!" Brawn bursts out. "Just let me at them!"

"Patience," says Optimus Prime. "You'll get your chance soon."

More than two dozen Autobots transform into their vehicular modes. Buster climbs into Beachcomber, and they all take off for the hills.

Turn to page 45, but be ready for action!

Cosmos and Sunstreaker meet Inferno on his way out of the Decepticons' lab. "We just found the button that controls the Destruction Beam!" he says happily. "Center City is safe!"

"And Megatron knows we're here, but he doesn't even care," Cosmos cries gleefully.

"Well, what do you think?" Cosmos asks. "Should we join the battle and finish off the rest of those rats?"

"Uh-uh, Cosmos," Inferno says. "I think we better get out of this fortress in a hurry."

"Why?" Cosmos asks, confused. It's not like Inferno to run away from an important fight. But Cosmos is already rushing to catch up with the other Autobots as they race outside. Soon they've all transformed and are zooming back toward headquarters, leaving the Decepticons' fortress behind them. In another instant, the fortress erupts in a blazing ball of fire that lights the sky for miles around.

"What was *that*?" cries Cosmos.

Inferno chuckles. "We not only stopped the Destruction Beam, we called it back to its origin. The Decepticons fell prey to their own evil invention!"

Cosmos sighs happily. "The humans need never fear them again!"

THE END

Sparkplug thinks for a moment. "You have no time to be tactful," he tells the Autobots. "The people of Center City are just going to have to deal with the concept of robots—or they're going to get creamed by the Destruction Beam."

Faster than lightning, the fleet of cars and trucks transforms into an army of sleek, powerful robots. Moving cautiously, the Autobots enter the city. They've got their eyes peeled for Decepticons, so they aren't concentrating on how the humans are reacting to them. They don't notice when a man driving a car stops to stare at them . . . and stares so long he causes a pile-up. They don't see the woman who, terrified of them, screams and drops an armload of groceries. But there are no Decepticons in sight.

"We better find the mayor," Optimus Prime announces. "We've got to evacuate the area."

The Autobots set out for City Hall. But they've gone only a few steps when hoards of policemen zoom through the city in patrol cars, making announcements with their bullhorns. "Attention!" they shout. "Center City is under siege by giant robots. Seek shelter, citizens. Repeat, seek shelter."

"Under siege by giant robots!" cries Optimus Prime. "Then the Decepticons *are* here!"

. . . .

Maybe you'll find them on page 63.

The Autobots in the lead team transform into their vehicular modes and head out along the main highway to Center City. They're going to stop Rumble and the other Decepticons who are preparing the area for the Destruction Beam with minor earthquakes. A smaller team of Autobots is heading for the fortress to try and knock out the beam itself.

The lead team travels at just above the speed limit. They'd love to step on the gas, but they can't risk attracting a lot of attention to themselves. Cosmos, the spaceship, is riding in back of Optimus Prime's trailer so that no humans will see him and panic. But Cosmos is completely miserable in the back of the truck and he tells Optimus Prime why. "If I can't even be out in the open now, on a deserted road, what can I possibly do in Center City? The people there would be terrified if they saw me," he says. "I'm turning back. I want to try and catch up with the others going to the fortress."

Optimus Prime pulls over to the shoulder of the road to have a little talk with Cosmos—a quick talk, of course, since the Destruction Beam is getting ever closer to Center City.

If you were Optimus Prime, what would you say to Cosmos?

. . . .

If you'd say, "Maybe you're right. You would be more useful as a spy at the fortress," turn to page 31.

If you'd say, "It's too dangerous to go after the others alone. You better stick with us," go on to page 37.

Reluctantly, Cosmos remains with the lead team of Autobots on their way to Center City. He gets back into Optimus Prime's storage section and they race down the highway to catch up with the others. The Autobots take a quick detour off the main road so they can pick up their human friend Sparkplug, the mechanic. Optimus Prime knows that when the Autobots get to Center City, they'll need someone who understands humans.

"What's going on?" Sparkplug asks as he jumps into Optimus Prime's cab. The Autobot leader quickly explains about the Destruction Beam.

The Autobots continue their journey and this time they do step on the gas pedal. About half a mile outside of Center City, they turn off the highway onto a deserted road and park in a grove of trees. Optimus Prime addresses his army.

"Autobots," he says, "we must enter the city immediately!"

"In our vehicular mode?" asks Cosmos. "We won't be able to do much."

"But our robot mode is frightening to humans," says Inferno, a fire truck.

"Sparkplug, you're a human," says Optimus Prime. "What do you think?"

Sparkplug's answer is going to effect the future of every living creature on the earth.

. . . .

If Sparkplug should tell the Autobots to enter Center City as robots, turn to page 34.

If he should tell them to enter as vehicles, turn to page 51.

The Decepticons spread out through their fortress, searching for the Autobots. In no time flat, they've captured Windcharger and Powerglide and drag them to Megatron's quarters.

"Prepare to die, foolish ones!" cries Megatron at the Autobots standing before him. "How dare you think you could deceive a ruler as great as I? Your folly will cost you dearly. You'll be only an unpleasant memory—and the same will be true for humankind in a few days! Buzzsaw, do away with these . . . . things. Choose something ghastly."

As the Autobots are led off, Megatron reaches for Beachcomber's communicator. "And now, a little present for Optimus Prime," he says.

Disguising his voice, he sends a short message. "All is well but we need backup. Come quickly." He transmits the fortress coordinates and waits to see if the Autobots will take the bait.

At Autobot headquarters, Optimus Prime receives the message and responds. "On our way," he radios back.

When the Autobots arrive, the Decepticons greet them at the cliff's hidden door with a full-scale attack.

"Surprise!" shouts Megatron.

The battle lasts only seconds. The Autobots are crushed before they know what hit them.

"The world is ours now," Megatron tells the Decepticons with wicked pleasure. "*All* ours. As for the earthlings, to use their own expression, their goose is cooked. Pretty soon, Decepticons, we shall feast!"

THE END

Megatron stands in the fortress corridor and glares at Cosmos. "Listen, twerp, there's absolutely nothing you could tell me that would give me more pleasure than blowing you away! Your flying days are over. I'll ground you permanently!" He reaches over and presses a tiny button on the wall. Instantly, Decepticons come running.

Cosmos tries his communicator again. He can't call the other Autobots for help, but he is able to send signals to them. Time is running out for him . . . . and for the world.

Just as Megatron is about to order Cosmos dismantled, the Autobot sees his buddy Red Alert running down the hall. Behind him is half the Autobot team. Cosmos guesses that the other half is gathering at the opposite end of the hall.

He's right. The Autobots have the Decepticons surrounded. They attack them, fighting fiercely. But the Decepticons far outnumber the Autobots. "We can't fight much longer!" Cosmos shouts to Red Alert. "This is taking up too much time. While we fight, the Destruction Beam is honing in on Center City!"

"Just what Megatron wants," replies Red Alert. "We're playing right into his hands."

There's no way to end the battle and escape. The Autobots stay and fight. The last Decepticon has just fallen when an ear-shattering roar rumbles through the corridors of the fortress . . . .

. . . .

Turn to page 67—if you dare.

39

The Autobot and Buster run desperately through the hallways of the enemy fortress and escape from the wounded Thrust. But Beachcomber is frantic. They have only twenty-five minutes before the Destruction Beam hits Center City.

Twenty minutes later, Beachcomber and Buster are heading down yet another hallway. They've had no luck finding either Jessie or the key to the Destruction Beam. And it doesn't look like Fortune is about to start smiling on them at this point either. Coming down the other end of the hallway are the Decepticons Starscream and Dirge.

Beachcomber and Buster whirl around, looking for some way to escape. Behind them are Megatron and Thrust, who seems to have recovered from his scrape with Beachcomber and Buster. The Autobot and the human stare at each other in horror. They're trapped, and in five minutes Center City is going to be just a beautiful memory!

Starscream pulls out his weapon and covers Beachcomber and Buster. The Decepticons and their two prisoners walk down the fortress hallways until they come to a small black door.

"Come into my lab," laughs Megatron. He opens the door and pushes Beachcomber and Buster into the room.

. . . .

Want to find out what twisted experiment awaits Beachcomber and Buster in the lab? Turn to page 7.

Desperately hoping to end the panic they've caused in Center City, the Autobots transform into vehicular mode. But by now they've run out of time.

Very softly, the ground beneath Center City begins to shake. The Destruction Beam has hit! Then, from behind a building, Rumble steps forward. He begins pounding his fists against the ground. Huge cracks open in the earth, swallowing up people and cars. Sections of road fall in. Buildings crumble and crash down in smoking, dusty heaps. Five Autobots are lost in a gaping fissure that suddenly appears in the ground.

Just as things begin to quiet down, a figure roars through the sky.

"That's Thundercracker," says Beachcomber sadly. "The Decepticons must be on their way here to make sure no one in Center City survives. It looks like the Autobots at the Decepticons' fortress failed, too."

Then the ground splits again as earthquake after earthquake tears the city apart. More Autobots and people fall helplessly into the depths of the earth. Then Optimus Prime himself falls in.

Above them, Megatron laughs wickedly. The Decepticons move into the ruins of Center City to make sure no one and nothing is left alive.

The most powerful Autobots are lost forever and, worst of all, Megatron has the whole world in his iron grip. Too bad humans haven't set up a moon station yet, because life on earth is going to be pretty unpleasant from now on.

THE END

The Autobots, armed with Sparkplug's sensible plan, speed into Center City and park in front of City Hall. "Wish me luck," says Sparkplug as he jumps out of Optimus Prime, but the Autobot leader doesn't answer. A talking truck would frighten the earthlings.

Inside City Hall, Sparkplug speaks urgently with Mayor Todd. "I tell you, Center City is right on the fault line. You've got to evacuate the people *now*."

Mayor Todd is convinced by what Sparkplug is saying. It's not really Sparkplug's words that convince him but the look of urgency tinged with fear in the mechanic's eyes. With one phone call from the mayor, every radio station in Center City is broadcasting earthquake warnings. But because there's a workable evacuation plan, the people don't panic. They gather peacefully in the streets, and soon the first group has been loaded into the Autobots. The vehicles make a quick trip to a campground outside the city. Cosmos hovers high in the sky so the people don't see him. He keeps a sharp watch for approaching Decepticons.

After four more trips, the Autobots are losing some power—but every single person in Center City has been evacuated. As Optimus Prime pulls into the campsite with his last load, Cosmos radios to him, "Decepticons approaching."

. . . .

Turn to page 44.

The Autobots see the Decepticons flying in, but they can't stop to fight. It is more important to carry the humans to safety.

The Autobots and humans watch as the buildings of Center City begin to quiver ever so slightly. The humans look at each other in bewilderment, but the Autobots know that the Destruction Beam has hit and made a deep crack in the foundation of the city—a crack just waiting to be split wide open by the Decepticons.

"I guess the others couldn't stop the beam," observes Beachcomber. "I wonder what that means."

"I don't know," admits Optimus Prime, "but let's unload the last of these humans and get to Center City. Maybe we can stop Rumble."

The humans can't believe their ears! Talking cars and trucks? But the Autobots don't have to worry about that now.

Turn to page 72.

The Autobots zoom toward the Decepticon fortress. Optimus Prime stops the convoy half a mile from its destination. "We're almost there," he announces. "This is our big chance. We can change the Decepticons into *Decrep-ticons*!"

"Yeah!" shouts Brawn.

"The Decepticons aren't expecting us," Optimus Prime continues. "We could storm the main entrance and move in on them in an offensive attack, or we could be sneakier and infiltrate the fortress quietly through the secret passage Buster found!"

"Quick!" says Buster. "The Destruction Beam is getting closer to Center City every second. There's no time to discuss this! Pick a number between one and ten."

If you chose an even number, turn to page 57.
If you chose an odd number, turn to page 54.

Beachcomber listens carefully so that he and Buster can follow the voices of the Decepticons and Jessie. He looks around the little cave just inside the fortress. A strip of light along the floor leaks out from underneath a door. Beachcomber feels around for the doorknob and pushes the door open a crack.

"Let me go!" Jessie shouts nearby.

Buster nudges Beachcomber. "Bingo!" he whispers.

Then they hear a cold, hollow voice silence Jessie. "Hush, human! You are now our prisoner, to do with as we please." The voices fade away.

Beachcomber pulls Buster into the wide, bright hall. Turning a corner several yards away are two Decepticons. One of them has Jessie slung over his shoulder, but she's struggling like mad. The Autobot and his human friend tiptoe behind them, hugging the rocky walls. Finally, the evil robots toss Jessie into a small, dim room, locking the metal door from the outside. "That ought to hold her," says one.

Jessie pounds furiously on the walls of her cell. The Decepticons stroll calmly down the hall. When they're out of sight, Beachcomber and Buster step up to Jessie's door.

Turn to page 70.

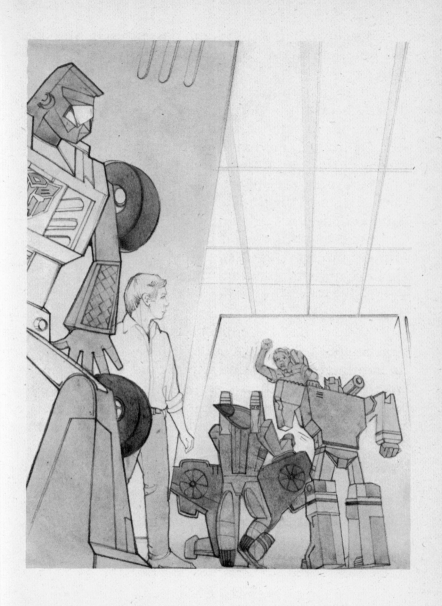

Beachcomber, Buster, and Jessie reach Autobot headquarters on the double. Mirage devises a brilliant plan.

In a few minutes, Mirage and Beachcomber are driving back to the Decepticons' fortress. They brake in front of the hideout, then sneak inside through the secret entrance. Finding a safe hiding place, Mirage projects his image at the end of the long corridor.

Buzzsaw, hurrying unsuspectingly down the hall, catches sight of the threatening image of Mirage. "An Autobot!" he cries.

Buzzsaw lunges—and the "Autobot" disappears. Mirage projects his image to another spot, then another, and yet another. "The fortress is overrun!" shouts Buzzsaw as he pushes an alarm button. "I've got to protect the lab!"

"Follow that Decepticon!" whispers Mirage to Beachcomber. They race after Buzzsaw and he leads them straight to the lab. Mirage and Beachcomber creep up behind him and quickly overpower the confused Decepticon. Pulling out their weapons, they blow Megatron's lab to bits and the Destruction Beam along with it.

"Now run for it!" shouts Beachcomber. As the Autobots race toward the fortress exit, they hear Megatron's harsh voice addressing the Decepticons. "An Autobot army attack. To your battle stations!"

Beachcomber grins. "Sometimes your worst enemy is your imagination."

THE END

Beachcomber and Buster hide inside the fortress until the voices of Jessie and the Decepticons fade away.

"Well, now what?" says Buster.

"How should I know?" replies Beachcomber. "You were the one who wanted to come back to the fortress and find Jessie. Now you think *I* should come up with a ready-made plan?"

Buster is quiet for a moment. "I know I've been calling the shots," he says sadly, "but I've drawn a blank. Please, you've got to do something. You're a robot. You have weapons."

"I am one robot against many," Beachcomber answers quietly. "The Decepticons have spent a lot of time developing their weapons. And they can fly. We're dealing with some very tough enemies, and your friend and your home city need us. We've got to work together or we'll fail. That would be a disaster. Are you with me?"

. . . .
Help Buster answer yes by turning to page 56.

Jessie grins evilly and glares at the captured Autobots and Buster. She walks over to Megatron. "Thank you, Great One," she says.

Buster lowers his head miserably. "Oh, no," he moans. "She's been brainwashed. She's on the Decepticons' side now."

Megatron takes the Autobots' communicators from them so that they can't signal for help. Then he sends Jessie out as a decoy to lead the other Autobots into Megatron's trap.

Optimus Prime remains silent. There's nothing he can do. He watches a radar screen in the lab and sees the Destruction Beam make contact with Center City. Megatron sees it, too. "Center City is now ready for Rumble's groundwaves. A few good waves and the city will crumble," the Decepticon gloats.

Megatron orders Starscream to lock up the Autobots and throw away the key. But, curiously enough, that's Optimus Prime's one hope. Megatron hasn't demanded that the Autobots be deactivated— they wouldn't be able to do a thing then. Maybe, just maybe, Optimus Prime can come up with a plan and escape. You'd better hope so. Otherwise, the entire world is about to come to . . . .

THE END

Sparkplug doesn't wait an instant before answering. "You can't go into Center City looking like robots! The people would go crazy with fear. Panic would spread, and in all the confusion you'd never be able to stop the Decepticons."

"But what good can we do as vehicles?" asks Beachcomber.

"Plenty," replies Sparkplug. "I'll talk with the mayor of the city. He's an old friend of mine. Somehow I'll convince him that we need to evacuate Center City. Then I'll provide him with the means for evacuation—you."

"The Autobots?" Optimus Prime says with surprise.

"Exactly. I can't think of any place humans would be safer than riding inside one of you."

"Well . . ." says Optimus Prime modestly.

"You'll have to make several trips, of course," Sparkplug continues, "but this plan should clear the roads of horrible traffic jams and keep the people from panicking. What do you say?"

"It sounds excellent to me," replies Optimus Prime. "In fact, I'm going to put it into action right now. Sparkplug, why don't you ride with me and we'll lead the way for the other Autobots."

Move out with the Autobots on page 43.

The three Autobots and the human turn left and hurry down yet another bleak hallway. Straight ahead of them is a huge door marked LAB.

"Something tells me that this isn't what it appears to be," says Beachcomber. He sends out a sensor. "You know what's behind that door? Air. A drop of at least one hundred feet. It's a trap."

"Hey," says Buster. "What's this?" He's found a small black doorway, almost invisible in the dim light.

"Probably the lab," says Optimus Prime. "Let's get some backup and find out." He pulls out his communicator and signals his coordinates. In a few moments, six more Autobots appear.

"Ready?" asks Optimus Prime. He takes aim with his laser rifle at the mysterious door and blasts it open. The Autobots and Buster rush into the room. They find themselves in a huge lab filled with equipment and machinery. And it's manned by three Decepticons!

But the Autobots are ready and the Decepticons have their hands full. *POW! POW! POW!* Brawn takes care of each Decepticon with a single blast.

And then, at that very moment, Megatron strides into the lab.

"Stay right where you are," says Optimus Prime softly. He's got his laser rifle trained on the Decepticon leader. "One move and I'll shatter you from here to Cybertron."

. . . .

Keep your eye on Megatron and turn to page 59.

The Autobots travel the last half-mile to the cliff that houses the Decepticons' fortress. Silently, they transform into their robot modes. "Okay, Buster," says Optimus Prime, "lead us to the entrance you found."

"This way," Buster whispers as he starts moving. The Autobots follow him through a long cavelike passage. At the end of it, Buster thumps his hand against what looks like a solid stone wall. A lever pops out, Buster presses it, and the rock wall swings open.

Buster turns to Optimus Prime. "This first room is just a little closet or something," he whispers. "Only a few of us can fit in it at one time. There's a door on the opposite side. When we go through that, we'll be in the main section of the fortress."

The Autobot leader nods. "Attack any Decepticons you see," he instructs the robots, "except Megatron. Capture him."

Beachcomber and Optimus Prime are the first to step out of the closet doorway. Optimus Prime signals for the others to enter the fortress, too. In a minute the Decepticons' hideout is completely breached. The Autobots break into groups of five or six and spread out through the fortress. Optimus Prime, Beachcomber, Buster, Brawn, and Sunstreaker make their way along a lighted hallway lined with locked doors on either side.

. . . .

Turn to page 71.

Turning right, the Autobots find that the long hallway they've chosen seems to lead nowhere. They walk and walk through the Decepticons' fortress, but they don't see any doors. At last they hear something. It's a faint voice, calling for help!

"That's Jessie!" cries Buster. "She can't be too far away. We've got to save her."

At the end of the hallway is a tall door. "She's in there!" says Optimus Prime. With one powerful blow, he breaks down the door and Jessie gratefully tumbles into Buster's arms.

"I know where the Decepticons' lab is!" exclaims Jessie. "Come on. Let's go and stop that Destruction Beam!"

The Autobots follow Jessie back through the hallway and around several corners. "In here," she says at last, pointing to a small red door.

The Autobots burst inside—and find themselves surrounded by Decepticons!

"There's no escape, Autobots," says Megatron. "Good work, Jessie."

Jessie?

Don't just sit there! Turn to page 50.

"All right, we can't hide forever," says Buster nervously. He glances around. He and Beachcomber seem to be in a dark, musty closet just inside the Decepticons' fortress. He feels along the rocky walls for a way out and his hand closes over a doorknob. Very slowly, he turns it. He inches the door open. Nothing. He opens it a bit more. Beachcomber is right behind him. Buster opens the door another fraction of an inch and —

BLAM!

The Decepticon Thrust is waiting on the other side of the door. He fires away, but Beachcomber and Buster just manage to dodge the bullets.

"I've got you now, vermin," Thrust says in a smooth, low voice as he backs the Autobots into the closet. "What a nice surprise you'll make for Megatron."

"Oh, yeah?" says Beachcomber. He plays the world's oldest trick on Thrust. Glancing over the Decepticon's shoulder into the hall beyond, he shouts, "It's all right now, Buster! Help is on the way!" Thrust turns around to face the imaginary enemy and Beachcomber and Buster push past him and race off, firing a few shots behind them as they run. One bullet glances off Thrust's metal head, stunning him.

Catch up with Buster and Beachcomber on page 40.

"All right!" cries Buster, taking charge. "We take the straightforward route. Those fortress doors are just standing there waiting for us."

"Let's hope that luck is on our side," says Beachcomber nervously.

The Autobots speed the rest of the way to the Decepticons' fortress. "Ready?" Optimus Prime asks when the Autobots are arranged in orderly rows in front of the evil hideout. "Prepare to attack the fortress!" he cries. "Transform!"

The Autobots transform into their robot mode and silently close ranks. Beachcomber stands in front of the massive double doors hidden in the cliff. They slide apart. . . .

Even though the fortress doors are wide open, Beachcomber doesn't move. He stares through the doors into the gloomy fortress. Then he turns to the waiting ranks of Autobots. "This is crazy," he says. "We shouldn't be fighting! Violence only leads to more violence!"

"Oh, no," groans Optimus Prime. "This is no time for an antiwar speech, Beachcomber. We've got to —"

"Drop your weapons!" booms a voice from within the dark depths of the fortress. "Every one of you stay where you are." It's Megatron. "We've got you covered with a mind-boggling arsenal of weapons!"

Turn to page 58.

Of course, the Autobots aren't about to give up their guns and be taken prisoner without a struggle. They fire madly as the evil robots pour out the doors of the fortress.

But the Decepticons are on familiar turf. Pretty soon, the Autobots are all either scrap metal or they've been taken prisoner.

"Well," Megatron says, turning to Thrust, "it looks like Evil has triumphed over Good yet again. The Destruction Beam should make contact shortly and then Rumble will send the city a few groundwaves to finish the job. Come," he says with an insane smile. "It's a lovely day to observe an earthquake."

The Decepticons go to Megatron's private observatory, where they watch Center City disappear in a colorful blue and purple cloud.

"This is only the beginning," Megatron declares. "When we turn the Destruction Beam on New York City, Peking, and Moscow, they'll crumble more beautifully!"

Whoever thought the end of the world would be a death-filled show for an alien robot gone haywire . . . ?

THE END

"All right," Optimus Prime demands, "how do I stop that Destruction Beam from hitting Center City?"

Megatron nods slightly toward the radar screen on the opposite side of the lab. "Press the red button," he instructs Optimus Prime.

Optimus Prime reaches out his hand but stops just before he hits the button. He's noticed the faintest smile on Megatron's face. "Forget it. That button is probably connected to a self-destruct mechanism."

"Too bad my trick didn't work," Megatron growls. "You'll never get me to tell you how to stop the Destruction Beam. Never!"

But Optimus Prime is watching Megatron and he sees that his enemy's gaze is resting on a metal lever on the wall across the room. "Hit that lever—fast!" he calls to Beachcomber.

In an instant, Beachcomber has flipped the switch to off. A blip on the radar screen halts in its path toward the bull's-eye.

"Victory!" cries Optimus Prime.

Actually, true victory doesn't come until a few hours later, when the Autobots defeat and deactivate all the Decepticons. They find Jessie tied up in a closet, dazed but unharmed.

The Autobots celebrate on their way back to headquarters by guzzling a few quarts of fine-grade oil. Buster and Jessie have super-fudge ice cream sundaes, instead.

THE END

Beachcomber watches Powerglide charge wreck-lessly down the brightly lit corridor of the Decepticon fortress. Windcharger heads for the storage room. Beachcomber shakes his head and looks around. All he can see are several closed doors and more deserted corridors. He can hear nothing at all. The fortress is eerily silent.

I've got to get at least a little more information for Optimus Prime, thinks Beachcomber. Cautiously he opens the door. Uh-oh! The Decepticon Dirge is waiting on the other side of the door! Beachcomber fires at him, but Dirge dodges neatly. "Child's play!" he cries. "When are you going to get a *real* weapon?"

"Not soon enough," says Beachcomber grimly.

Dirge lunges at Beachcomber and stuns him with a concussion missile. Then he removes the Autobot's right arm, his left arm, and finally his legs. "Hmm. These will make a . . . decent Decepticon." Finally, Dirge removes Beachcomber's memory tape and plays the last fifteen minutes.

"So," says Dirge, "he's not the only one here. Well, we'll take the power out of Powerglide and the wind out of Windcharger in no time flat."

Dirge flips open his communicator: "Megatron! We have company!"

Megatron, the evil ruler of the Decepticons, listens grimly to Dirge's news. "Find the other Autobots," he orders furiously.

. . . .
You better do what he says! Turn to page 38.

Staying hidden behind the boulders, Beach-comber transforms into his robot mode, then steps boldly in front of the cliff face into which Rumble just disappeared. *What's going to happen?* he wonders. *Will the doors open for me or remain shut tight?*

Much to Beachcomber's surprise, the doors immediately slide apart smoothly. Inside it's dark. Beachcomber sees a dim light and hears faint humming sounds. Hesitantly, he steps forward.

But suddenly, when he's only halfway through the doors, Beachcomber's sharp ears detect noises coming from the other side of the cliff. They sound like human voices. Are the humans working with the Decepticons? Beachcomber shudders. It's a horrible thought. He's sure he ought to investigate the sounds. But the doors are starting to close. If he leaves now, will they open for him again? Is this his last chance to check out the fortress? He has a big decision to make and very little time.

Quick! What should Beachcomber do?

. . . .

If you think Beachcomber should forget the fortress and investigate the voices, turn to page 21 . . . . and keep your fingers crossed.

If you think he should run into the fortress before the doors close, and leave the sounds behind him, hurry up and turn to page 14.

After the police announce that giant robots are attacking Center City, people begin to panic. Uselessly, they run screaming through the streets, ignoring the warning to seek shelter. In a matter of minutes, the roads leading out of the city are jammed. Traffic is at a standstill. Inside skyscrapers, the elevators get stuck as everyone tries to escape at once.

Optimus Prime looks at Beachcomber and Sparkplug in confusion. "We'll never find the mayor now," he says. "And by the way, where are the Decepticons? They're causing this mess, but we haven't seen one of them."

But something has just occurred to Cosmos. "Hey," he says, "I think *we're* causing the panic. Earthlings have never seen robots as big as us before."

. . . .

The adventure continues on page 42.

The three Autobots step into a dark, clammy cave. Beachcomber leads the others along a rocky passageway that seems to go on forever. Finally, the Autobots emerge into a shadowy space that looks like a storage room. On one side there's a door, and on the other there's a second passageway like the one they've just been in.

Beachcomber motions for Powerglide and Windcharger to keep quiet. He crosses the storage area and pauses by the door. There's a complicated lock on it, but that's no problem for Beachcomber. Skillfully, he picks it and pushes the door open. The Autobots tiptoe through and find themselves at the end of a long, brightly lit corridor. It is absolutely silent. The smell of evil is unmistakable.

"Okay," whispers Powerglide, "I'm gonna investigate the corridor."

"Not me! There's trouble brewing here," declares Windcharger. "I can feel it. *I'm* going back into the storage room to see what's down that other passageway."

Beachcomber looks from one Autobot to the other. Frankly, both plans scare him. But he knows he has to do *something*. Many lives may depend on it.

If you were Beachcomber, what would you do?

. . . .

If you'd head off with Windcharger, turn to page 11.

If you'd team up with Powerglide, turn to page 20.

If you'd go off on your own and check out some other parts of the fortress, turn to page 60.

64

"Come on," Windcharger says impatiently, "we're never going to solve that code. Let's get through the door some other way."

"Do you want to smash it down?" asks Beachcomber.

"You betcha." Windcharger gathers his strength and sends out a magnetic force field, but even his super-strong powers can't budge the door.

"Wow," he says, drained of energy. "I wonder what it's made of."

"I don't know," answers Beachcomber, "but you just made an awful lot of noise. I think we'd better get out of here."

The Autobots turn and rush back through the passageway. Behind them, the door swings open on silent hinges. Megatron, the Decepticon ruler, steps through it, sees the fleeing Autobots, and retreats into the room once again.

Seconds later, the Autobots near the storage area. They round a corner—and come face to face with Megatron in his weapon form.

· ·

Uh-oh! Turn to page 66.

As a nuclear-charged fusion cannon, Megatron takes aim . . . and shoots Beachcomber and Windcharger. When he finishes, there's not much left.

Powerglide has even worse luck than his two friends. The Decepticons capture him as he's roaming about the fortress. With a few quick changes in his circuitry, they force him to lead them to Autobot headquarters.

Although the Autobots are not expecting an attack, they fight well. Still, they weren't prepared for battle and, one by one, they fall. At last, only Optimus Prime is left.

"Come, my friend," Megatron says demoniacally. "I will not kill you, I will just . . . alter you a bit. I have a little job for you to do. It involves the destruction of earth's cities. You will be a powerful new ally to the Decepticon cause . . ."

The noble Optimus Prime would never submit to Megatron's evil—not even to save his own life. With a last effort of his will, Optimus Prime reaches for a small black button hidden above the doorway and—*KA-BOOM!!*—all of Autobot headquarters goes up in a giant explosion, taking Megatron and the evil Decepticons with it.

THE END

As the deafening roar dies down, Cosmos, Red Alert, and the rest of the Autobots race to the fortress entrance and look out. In the east, they see a huge bluish cloud of dust rising toward the sky. It's all that's left of Center City.

Cosmos is sure that the lead team of Autobots there fought Rumble and the other Decepticons bravely. Still, there was nothing they could do once the Destruction Beam reached its destination. And when the earth opened up and every building in Center City crumbled, the Autobots also slid into the gaping holes in the ground.

But there's a happy side to the story, too. Back at the fortress, the Autobots are in control. Cosmos somberly destroys the lab. "The destruction of the Destruction Beam! That's the end of Megatron's plan," he says.

"But we didn't wipe out all the Decepticons, and Center City is destroyed," Powerglide reminds him.

"That's true," agrees Cosmos, "but we saved the world and we got rid of a bunch of powerful enemies too! It's going to be much harder for Megatron to mess around with the earthlings now that he doesn't have a lab anymore. Now let's get of here and back to headquarters. This war with the Decepticons isn't over yet. In fact, it's just beginning. . . ."

THE END

The lead team of Autobots streams through the hills toward the Decepticons' fortress to stop the Destruction Beam at its source. Cosmos, the spaceship, flies excitedly above them. A smaller group heads for Center City to battle Rumble and any Decepticons who might be there with him.

It doesn't take long for the lead team to reach the fortress. As Optimus Prime pulls to a stop, he cries, "We're going to storm the place! Beachcomber, stand in front of the entrance you found. When the doors open, Brawn will keep them apart. The rest of you rush in. Disable any Decepticons you find, but top priority is locating the lab and figuring out how to stop the Destruction Beam. Ready? Autobots, transform!"

The heavy doors open easily for Beachcomber and, as Brawn holds them apart, the Autobots run into the fortress. The Decepticons immediately try to get into attack formation, but the Autobots disable them one by one.

In the heat of the battle, Optimus Prime maims Megatron himself with a laser rifle shot in the forearm. He grabs the Decepticon ruler around the neck. "Take me to your lab!" he shouts. "And if we're not there in two minutes, another laser shot will finish you off!"

Wordlessly, Megatron leads Optimus Prime down a long corridor. Beachcomber and Inferno follow. Behind them the battle rages.

. . . .

For the real action turn to page 30.

68

"Jessie," Buster whispers, his face pressed against the door of the fortress cell.

"Buster?" asks Jessie. "What took you so long?"

"That's gratitude for you!" says Buster to Beachcomber. "Okay. Stand back, Jessie. We're busting in!" The Autobot and the human slam into the door. "Ow!" Buster yells. The door doesn't budge.

Beachcomber uses his sensors to test the composition of the door. "Pure steel," he announces. He pulls out a pocket-size laser. "This ought to take care of the job." *ZAP!* The beam flashes out, slashing through the steel. *ZAP! ZAP! ZAP!* Beachcomber cuts a square in the metal door, just large enough for Jessie. He and Buster push the piece out and Jessie crawls through.

"Finally!" Jessie exclaims. "Okay, now we've got to find the lab. I heard the Decepticons talking. They control the Destruction Beam from there. If we can find it and figure out which button is hooked up to the beam, we'll be able to save Center City!"

Beachcomber, Buster, and Jessie dash through the mazelike corridors of the fortress, but ten minutes later they haven't seen a single sign of the lab. Beachcomber pulls the humans into an empty room and whispers, "I feel like we're searching for an invisible lab. I think we should give up and go get help. If we don't, Center City will be a thing of the past!"

. . . .

Don't waste a second before you turn to page 48.

"Before we find Jessie, I think we'd better find the Decepticons' lab," says Optimus Prime. "Megatron can probably control the Destruction Beam from there. Remember, we don't have much time before it is supposed to hit Center City."

Suddenly—*BLAM! BLAM! KA-BOOM!*

The Autobots have run into the Decepticons Skywarp, Ramjet, and Buzzsaw, their weapons drawn and firing. And the Decepticons definitely have the edge of surprise over the Autobots. They are letting loose with their cannons and missiles.

But Optimus Prime aims his laser rifle. Just as he pulls his trigger, the Decepticons also fire their weapons. The noise is deafening. When it dies down, the three Decepticons are lying incapacitated on the floor. So is Sunstreaker.

"We have to leave him," says Optimus Prime sadly.

The Autobots and Buster reach the end of the hallway, where it branches into two passageways. "Well, what do you think? Should we turn right or left?" asks Buster, looking around.

Since there's no logical way to make this choice, you might as well flip a coin.

. . . .

If the coin comes up heads, take the right passageway and turn to page 55.

If you get tails, go left and turn to page 52.

The Autobots move out. In Center City, they transform so that they're ready for battle. The first Decepticons they see are Rumble and Ramjet, who are there to start the earthquake. Optimus Prime makes quick work of them with his laser rifle. As other Decepticons move in, the Autobots pick them off with their weapons. Since the Decepticons are caught unaware, the battle is not too difficult. The fault line remains under Center City, but the earthquake is avoided.

"Now for the fortress," cries Optimus Prime. "And we'll finish the job!"

The Autobots drive past the campground, heading for the fortress. As they do, they transform for an instant into their robot mode. The humans are astonished, but not afraid. They cheer the mighty heroes on as the Autobots set out to achieve a final victory over the forces of evil.

THE END